No Such Thing

To my sister, Laurie, with love
—J. F. K.

For Seraphina Dilcher
—B. L.

Text copyright © 1997 by Jackie French Koller
Illustrations copyright © 1997 by Betsy Lewin

Published by Caroline House
Boyds Mills Press, Inc.
A Highlights Company
815 Church Street
Honesdale, Pennsylvania 18431
Printed in Mexico

Publisher Cataloging-in-Publication Data
Koller, Jackie French.
No such thing / by Jackie French Koller ; illustrated by Betsy Lewin.
—1st ed.
[32]p. : col.ill. ; cm.
Summary : A boy is afraid there is a monster under his bed, until he meets a monster
who is afraid there is a boy above *his* bed.
ISBN 1-56397-490-8
1. Monsters—Fiction—Juvenile literature. 2. Bedtime—Fiction—Juvenile literature.
[1. Monsters—Fiction. 2. Bedtime—Fiction.] I. Lewin, Betsy, ill. II. Title.
[E]—dc20   1997   AC   CIP
Library of Congress Catalog Card Number 96-83929

First edition, 1997
Book designed by Tim Gillner
The text of this book is set in 16-point Melior.
The illustrations are done in pen and ink and watercolors.

10 9 8 7 6 5 4 3 2 1

No Such Thing

by Jackie French Koller

Illustrated by Betsy Lewin

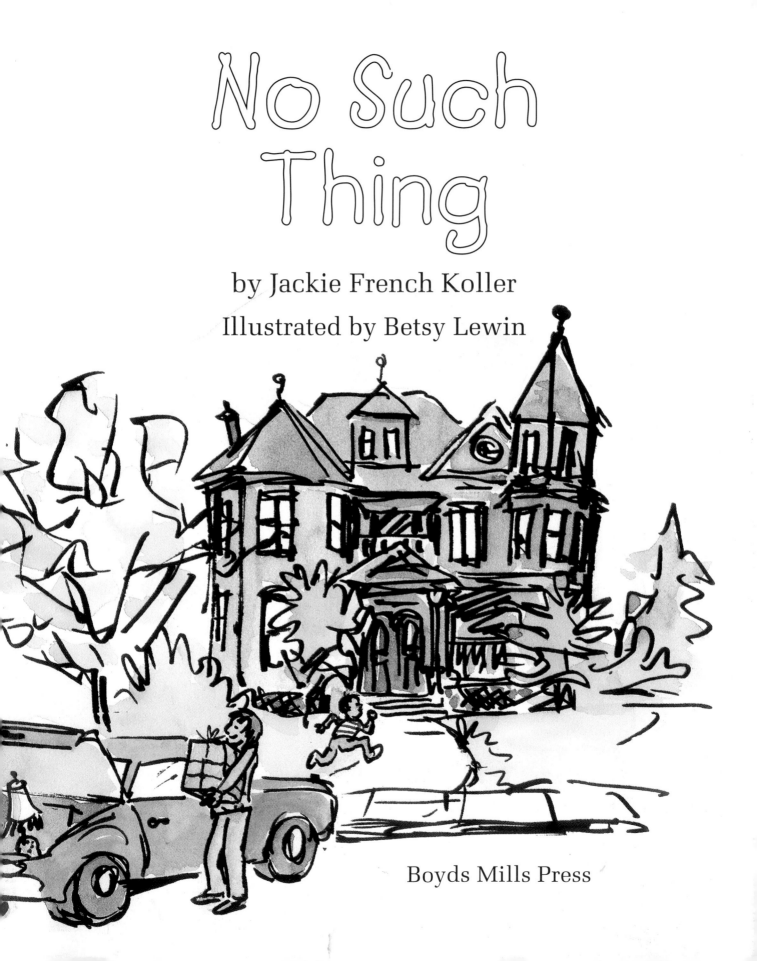

Boyds Mills Press

H

oward loved the old house he and his family had just moved into. He loved all the neat little nooks and crannies, and the large windows that nearly touched the floor. He couldn't wait to explore all the funny little closets and cupboards.

He even liked his big, old-fashioned bed.

Until it got dark . . .

"I think there's a monster under my bed," Howard told his mommy when she came in to kiss him goodnight.

Howard's mommy laughed. "This old house is playing tricks with your imagination," she said. "You know there are no such things as monsters. Now, be a good boy and go to sleep."

Monster's mommy came in to kiss *him* goodnight.
"I think there's a boy on top of my bed,"
Monster told her.

Monster's mommy sniggled. "Oh, Monster," she said, "you know there are no such things as boys. Go to sleep now."

Howard heard a snurkle.

"Mommy," he cried, "come quick!"

"What is it Howard?" his mommy asked.

"There *is* a monster," said Howard. "I heard him snurkling under my bed."

Howard's mommy laughed again. "You've been watching too many scary movies, Howard," she said. "I told you, monsters are only make believe."

Monster heard a sneeze.

"Mommy, come quick!" he called.

"What is it, Monster?" his mommy asked.

"There *is* a boy," said Monster. "I heard him sneezing on top of my bed."

Monster's mommy sniggled again. "You've been reading too many comic books, Monster," she said. "I told you, boys are only pretend."

Howard peeked over the edge of his bed.

"Mommy, come quick!" he cried.
"I can see his tail!"

Howard's mommy rushed into his room.
She picked Howard's jump rope off the floor.

"Howard," she said. "I'm losing patience.
Tail indeed!"

Monster peeked out from under the bed.
"Mommy, come quick!" he called.
"I can see his fingers!"
Monster's mommy came in. She didn't see anything.
"I'm sure it was just your pet tarantula,"
she told Monster. "Now, go to sleep!"

Howard decided to take one more look.

Monster decided to take one more look.

Howard ran to get his mommy. "He's there!
He's there!" he cried. "I saw him looking up at me!"

Monster went running to get his mommy.
"He's there! He's there!" he shouted.
"I saw him looking down at me!"

Monster's mommy took him back to his room.
She lifted him up to see the top of the bed.
"There," she said. "Now are you satisfied?"

Howard's mommy took him back to his room.
She knelt on the floor with him to look under the bed.
"There," she said. "Are you satisfied now?"

Howard's mommy tucked him in once more.
"Now, this is it, Howard," she said. "If I have to
come in here again, you are going to be punished.
Good night!"

Monster's mommy tucked him in once more.
"I've had it, Monster," she said. "If I have to come in here again, you are going to be twaddled. Now, go to sleep!"

Howard put his face in his pillow and started to cry. He cried and cried.

Monster pulled his spider web over his face and started to whimple. He whimpled and whimpled.

Between sobs, Howard heard a strange sound.
It sounded sad.

Between whimples, Monster heard a strange sound.
It sounded scared.

Howard peeked over the edge of the bed. A very sad
face looked up at him.

Monster peeked out from under the bed.
A very scared face looked down at him.

"Were you crying?" Monster asked.

"Yes," said Howard. "Were you whimpling?"

"Yes," said Monster.

"Why?" asked Howard.

"Because I'm scared of you," said Monster. "Boys eat little monsters."

"Eat little monsters!" Howard tumbled back on his bed and laughed. He laughed and laughed. "Where did you get a silly idea like that?" he asked. "Boys don't eat monsters!"

"They don't?" asked Monster.

"Of course not," said Howard. Then he stopped laughing. "But *monsters* eat *boys*. Are you going to eat me?"

Monster started to sniggle. He sniggled so hard that he rolled back on the floor and kicked his feet in the air.

"Monsters eat boys!" he cried. "That's the funniest thing I ever heard. Where did you get such a crazy idea? Did your mommy tell you that?"

"No," said Howard. "My mommy says there are no such things as monsters."

Monster stopped laughing.

    "Really?" he said. "My mommy says there are
no such things as boys. She never believes me
when I hear boy noises at night."

    "I know," said Howard. "Mine never believes
me either."

    Howard and Monster sat slowly shaking
their heads, when suddenly Howard started to smile.

    "Come here," he said.

    He leaned close and whispered in Monster's ear.
Monster sniggled and nodded.

    Monster crawled *on top* of the bed.

    Howard crawled *under* the bed.

    "Oh, Mommy," they both called together.
"Mommy, come quick!"